William Forbes-Leith

Life of St. Margaret, Queen of Scotland

William Forbes-Leith

Life of St. Margaret, Queen of Scotland

ISBN/EAN: 9783743345904

Manufactured in Europe, USA, Canada, Australia, Japa

Cover: Foto ©Raphael Reischuk / pixelio.de

Manufactured and distributed by brebook publishing software
(www.brebook.com)

William Forbes-Leith

Life of St. Margaret, Queen of Scotland

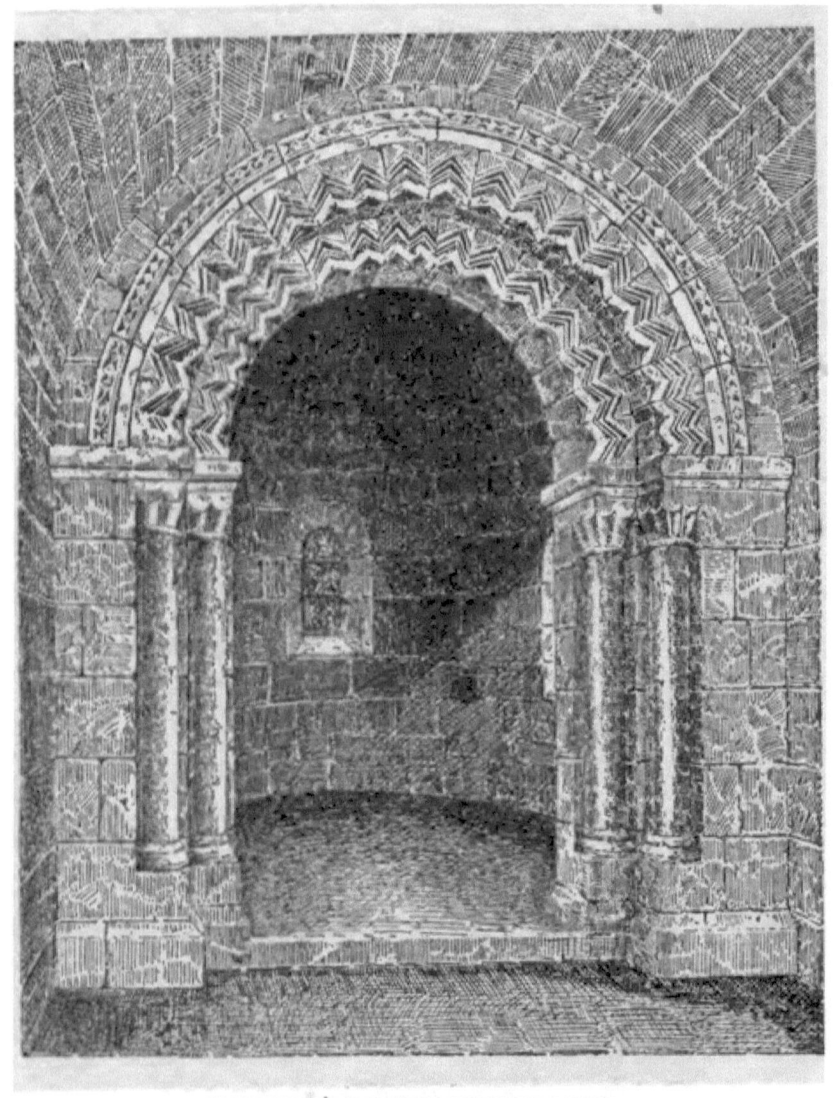

ST MARGARET'S ORATORY IN EDINBURGH CASTLE.

OF

ST. MARGARE

QUEEN OF SCOTLAND

BY

TURGOT, BISHOP OF ST ANDREWS

Translated from the Latin by

WILLIAM FORBES-LEITH, S.J.

THE FRATERY OF DUNFERMLINE ABBEY.

EDINBURGH: WILLIAM PATERSON

MDCCCLXXXIV

CONTENTS.

CHAPTER III.

CHAPTER IV.

ILLUSTRATIONS.

The Royal Palace appears to have been much enlarged and thoroughly repaired about 1540. Large mullioned windows were introduced into the original architecture. The present upper storey with bay windows was then added to the building. , The west wall overlooking the glen is 205 feet in length.

In 1250 the remains of St Margaret were transferred from the old original tomb, in the now western church, to the splendid new tomb specially erected to receive them in the "Lady Aisle" of the then recently-built choir. From 1250 to 1560, *lights* were kept perpetually burning before this tomb, as also on each side of the shrine, of which frequent mention is made in the *Register of Dunfermline*. This tomb appears to have been destroyed by the reformers on the 28th of March, 1560, or by the falling of the walls shortly after that period. All that now remains is the double plinth of a limestone, in dilapidated condition, now outside the area of the present church (on the east). On the upper plinth are still to be seen six circular indentures, from which rose "*six slender shafts of shapely stone*," that supported a highly-ornamented canopy. In the centre of the second or upper plinth stood St Margaret's shrine. (*E. Henderson*, "*Annals of Dunfermline*," p. 86.)

VIGNETTES.

It is situated but a short distance up the glen from the royal abode. According to tradition, St Margaret often resorted there for private devotion. The custom of retiring for a time to a cave was very common among the British and Scottish Saints. (*Cf.* "*Historians of Scotland,*" vol. v., p. 345.)

INTRODUCTION.

THE great loss sustained by the English in the death of Harold was their deprivation of a national leader. Harold's brothers had fallen with him in the field at Senlac. Of his sons no mention was ever made. Once more men looked to the royal line, and the Ætheling Edgar, the grandson of Edmund Ironside, whilst still a boy, was chosen king. Such a leader did but weaken the national cause; and no sooner did William approach the city of London than all opposition faded away. The northern Earls, Edwin and Morkar, would hazard nothing, and, dismayed by William's advance, made haste to retreat northwards. The bishops, after a brief display of resistance, counselled submission to him, and at Christmas his coronation finally made him King of England.

Thus ended the Saxon's main struggle for freedom. But the country was by no means conquered. East of a line from Norwich to Dorset, William was king. All north and west of that was yet to be won. The English, however, felt that they were almost conquered, and the schemes they formed for their deliverance were wild and desperate. The signal for a general revolt came from Swegen, King of Denmark, on the appearance of his fleet in the Humber in 1068. All northern, western, and south-western England rose as one man. The outbreak was heralded by the storming of York, and by the slaughter of three thousand Normans who formed its garrison. The news of this massacre reached William as he was hunting in the forest of Dean, and, in a wild outburst of wrath, he swore to avenge himself on the North. But wrath went hand-in-hand with the coolest statesmanship. The real enemies to be disposed of were the Danes. These William bought off, and then turning upon the disorganised rebels, he defeated them in detail by a series of masterly marches. The English submitted, and left the Normans undisputed masters of the kingdom. Edgar the Ætheling, with his mother Agatha, his sisters Margaret and Christina, and the last relics of the English nobility,[1] resolved to sail for Wearmouth, and to seek a shelter at the court of Malcolm, King of Scotland. They could hardly have expected to find the man who was to have been their host, in the very act of ravaging

---

[1] These were the English Thanes : Archill, the great Northumbrian Thane, to whom Malcolm granted large territories in Dumbarton, compensating the spoliation he had sustained from the Conqueror : Merlesweyn, Siward-Barn, Alfwin, all of whom can be recognised as landed men under Malcolm, and whose descendants subsequently appear high on the roll of Scotland's territorial aristocracy. Tradition also mentions the families of Lyndesay, Vaux, Ramsey, Lovel, Towers, Preston, Sandiland, Wisheart, Soulis, Maxwell, Crichton, Giffard, Maule, Leslie and Borthwick, established in the Scottish dominions during Malcolm's reign. (Sir Francis Palgrave, " History of England and Normandy," vol. iv., p. 335. Cf. Hailes, " Ann. Scot.," vol. i., pp. 7, 8 : the " Scots Compendium," etc.)

their native country; but his savage occupa-
tion in no way lessened his friendly feelings
towards them. He met them in person, he
gave them the most hearty reception, and bade
them dwell in his realm as long as it might
please them.[1] They sailed towards Scotland; he
went on with the harrying of Northumberland.
For while he was still at Wearmouth, news had
been received that Gospatric, William's earl in
Northumberland, had burst into Malcolm's
Cumbrian province, had devastated the land with
fire and sword, and had returned with great spoil
to the old fortress of the Northumbrian kings at
Bambrough, which he held as his headquarters.
When the news of Gospatric's inroad into
Cumberland was brought to Malcolm, he was

---

[1] Edgar and his suite were not unknown to the Scottish
king. Deprived of his father's protection in early youth
"Malcolm grew up into manhood under the Confessor's
benign protection, his benefactor and his suzerain, standing
before the Confessor's throne, consorting with the Confessor's
knights, sitting at the Confessor's table." (Sir Francis
Palgrave, "History of England and Normandy," vol. iv.,
p. 311.)

filled with wrath, and issued orders such as William never gave. From that day forward none of English race were to be spared; the remnant that the Norman had left were to pay for the exploit of their Earl by death or hopeless slavery. The word was given, and it was carried out to the letter by the ruthless marauders to whom it was addressed. The old men and women were slaughtered, as Simeon of Durham puts it, like swine for the banquet.[1] Young men and maidens, and all who were of age and strength to be useful in slavery, were driven in fetters to the land of bondage.[2] Many sank through fatigue, some of them never to rise again; those in whom life was left found no pity, but were driven on all the more unsparingly at the ruthless bidding of Malcolm. Thus, we are told, was Scotland filled with English slaves of either sex. There was not a village, there was not even a house so poor but could boast of some English captive held in thraldom.[3]

[1] " Simeonis Dunelmensis Opera," p. 88, Surtees Society.
[2] *Ibid.* [3] *Ibid.*

While Malcolm was thus making his fearful march homewards, rich with the human spoil of noble England, the English exiles had reached Scotland in safety by sea. Some of the party soon returned to share the dangers of the insurgents at Ely.[1] But the Ætheling and his family paid Malcolm a longer visit, and Margaret, the sister of Edgar, was now entreated by the King to accept his hand. Both the sisters of Edgar, however, were inclined to a religious life.[2] Margaret, her brother and all her companions, at the first utterly refused to hearken to the king's suit. But the love of Malcolm was not to be withstood. " He dealt with her brother till he said Yea; for in truth he durst not say otherwise, seeing they had come into Malcolm's power."[3] "It was," says Mr Freeman, "a good day for Malcolm and for Scotland when Margaret was

---

[1] Freeman, " History of the Norman Conquest," vol. iv., p. 468.

[2] Christina became Abbess of an English monastery.

[3] " Chron. Wig.," 1067. The marriage took place about 1070. Cf. E. Freeman, vol. iv., appendix B.B., p. 782.

persuaded or constrained to exchange the easy self-dedication of the cloister for the harder task of doing her duty in that state of life to which it had pleased God to call her.[1] Margaret became the mirror of wives, mothers, and queens, and none ever more worthily earned the honours of Saintship. Her gentle influence reformed whatever needed to be reformed in her husband, and none laboured more diligently for the advance of temporal and spiritual enlightenment in her adopted country. . . . There was indeed no need for Margaret to bring a new religion into Scotland, but she gave a new life to the religion which she found existing there. She became the correspondent of Lanfranc, and her life was written by the

---

[1] No royal marriage was ever more important in its results for England. " It was through Margaret that the old kingly blood of England passed into the veins of the descendants of the Conqueror. The tree returns to the root when Henry the First marries Matilda the daughter of Margaret; it bears leaves at the birth of her children." (E. Freeman, " History of the Norman Conquest," vol. iii., p. 12.)

holy Prior and Bishop Turgot.[1] It is one of the most interesting pieces that we have as a personal and ecclesiastical biography."[2] As one of our most distinguished Scotch writers truly observes :—" There is perhaps no more beautiful character recorded in history than that of Margaret. For purity of motives, for an earnest desire to benefit the people among whom her lot was cast, for a deep sense of religion and great personal piety, for the unselfish performance of whatever duty lay before her, and for entire self-abnegation, she is unsurpassed, and the chroniclers of the time[3] all bear testimony to her exalted character."[4]

Turgot's Memoir of St Margaret is the only authentic account we have of her life. "My

[1] Turgot, Prior of Durham, was consecrated Bishop of St Andrews at York on the 1st August 1109; he died on 31st of August 1115.

[2] E. Freeman, "History of the Norman Conquest," vol. iv. p. 510.

[3] "Orderic Vital," b. viii. c. 20; "Anglo-Saxon Chronicle," Thorpe's edition, vol. ii. p. 172.

[4] W. F. Skene, "Celtic Scotland," vol. ii. p. 344.

evidence," says Turgot, "is especially trust-worthy, since (thanks to her great and familiar intercourse with me) I am acquainted with the most part of her secrets." As the late Dr Forbes truly remarks, "there is an atmosphere of calm unexcited truthfulness about the narrative, as well as an absence of the mythical, which commends it to us as the work of an eminent truth-loving man, and the incidental allusions to the current history bear the test of all that we know of the times."[1]

It is also "full of instructive notices of the state of the Scottish Church and kingdom at the epoch of the Norman conquest of England, and *it supplies us with the first really authentic history of Scotland* after the notices in Adamnan and Bæda, The Pictish Chronicle, and the Book of Deer."[2]

For the following translation of the life gene-

[1] Dr A. Penrose Forbes, "Calendars of the Scottish Saints," p. 390.

[2] *Ibid.*, p. 386.

rally ascribed to Turgot we have used the Latin text printed in the *Acta Sanctorum*, vol. ii., 101 (10th June). Papebroch, who edited it, contends that it was written by Theodoric. His arguments, however, do not seem to us very conclusive. According to Lord Hailes, and other writers, it is probable that Theodoric is either another name for Turgot, or that the name of Theodoric has been prefixed to the Saint's life instead of Turgot by some copier.[1]

[1] Of the "Life of Queen Margaret" but one copy exists in manuscript in this kingdom, in a folio volume on vellum, of the latter part of the twelfth century, Cotton, Tiberius, D. III., which was much injured by the great fire in the British Museum. The same life is printed in the *Acta Sanctorum*, in Pinkerton's Lives of Scottish Saints, in the publications of the Surtees Society (1868). An abridgment exists in in the MS. Cotton. Tiberius, E. 1, a folio in double columns, also injured by fire, and dates from the beginning of the fourteenth century.

On the question of the authorship of this work, see the preface to "Simeonis Dunelmensis Opera," Surtees Society, 1868.

THE PROLOGUE.

TO the honourable and excellent Matilda, queen of the English, T[urgot],[1] servant of the servants of St Cuthbert, sends the blessing of peace and health in this present life, and in that which is to come the chief good of all good things.

§ 1. You have, by the request you made to me, commanded me (for a request of yours is to me a command) to offer you in writing the story of the life of your mother, whose memory is held in veneration. How acceptable that life was to God you have often heard by the concordant praise of many. You remind me how in this matter my evidence is especially trustworthy, since (thanks to her great and familiar intercourse with me) you have understood that I am

---

[1] *Theodericus* in the "Acta Sanctorum," and in Pinkerton's edition. In the Cotton. MS., at the end of the paragraph, there are added, in a hand of the seventeenth century, *Per Turgotum Dunelmensem.*

acquainted with the most part of her secrets. These your commands and wishes I willingly obey; nay, more, I venerate them exceedingly, and I respectfully congratulate you—whom the King of the Angels has raised to the rank of Queen of England—on this, that you desire not only to hear about the life of your mother, who ever yearned after the Kingdom of the Angels, but further, to have it continually before your eyes in writing, in order that, although you were but little familiar with her face, you might at least have a perfect acquaintance with her virtues.

For my part, my own wish inclines me to do what you bid, but I have, I do own, a lack of ability: as the materials forsooth for this undertaking are more than my writing or my words can avail to set forth.

§ 2. So I am in two minds and drawn two ways at once. On the one hand, the greatness of the subject makes me shrink from obeying; on the other, I dare not refuse because of the authority of you who command me, and the memory of her of whom I am to speak. I cannot do justice to my subject, but my duty is to make it known so far as I can. I owe this to the love I have for her, and to the obedience which is due from me to you. I trust that the grace of the Holy Spirit, which gave her such powers for good, will to me vouchsafe also the ability to recount them. "The Lord shall give the word to them that preach good tidings with great power." (Ps. lxvii. 12.)[1]

§ 3. In the first place, then, it is my wish that you should know, and others through you, that were I to attempt to recount all I could tell to her honour, it might be thought that, under cover of your mother's praises, I was flattering your own queenly dignity. But far be it from my grey hairs to mingle falsehood with the virtues of such a woman as she was, in unfolding which I profess—as God is my Witness and my Judge—that I add nothing to the truth. On the contrary, I suppress many things, fearing that they might appear incredible, and I might be charged (as the orator says) with decking out the crow in the plumage of the swan.

---

[1] "Open thy mouth wide, and I will fill it," (Ps. lxxxvii. 10). "For no one can fail in the Word who believes in the Word." "In the beginning was the Word, and the Word was God." (St John i. 1.)

ST MARGARET'S TOMB, DUNFERMLINE ABBEY.

CHAPTER I.

§ 4.

MANY, as we read, have got their name from a quality of their mind, so that in their regard there is shown a correspondence between the word of their name and the grace they have received. Peter was so named from " the Rock," that is Christ, in token of the firmness of his faith ; John, which means " the grace of God," from his contemplation of the Divinity, and his prerogative of Divine love; and the sons of Zebedee were styled Boanerges, that is, " the sons of thunder," because they thundered forth the preaching of the Gospel. The same thing was true of this virtuous woman, for the fairness which was pre-shadowed in her name was eclipsed by the surpassing beauty of her

soul. She was called Margaret, and in the sight
of God she showed herself to be a pearl, precious
in faith and works. She was indeed a pearl to
you, to me, to all of us, yea, to Christ Himself, and being Christ's she is all the more ours
now that she has left us, having been taken
to the Lord. This pearl, I repeat, has been
removed from the dunghill of the present world,
and now she shines in her place among the
jewels of the Eternal King. Of this no one,
I think, will doubt, who reads the following
narrative of her life and death. When I call to
mind her conversations with us, seasoned as they
were with the salt of wisdom; when I bethink
me of her tears wrung from the compunction of
her heart; when I regard her staidness and the
even balance of her manners; when I remember
her affability and prudence, I rejoice while I
lament, and in lamenting I rejoice. I rejoice,
because she has passed away to God, after whom
she yearned; and I grieve because I am not
rejoicing along with her in the heavenly places.
I rejoice for her, because she now sees, in the
land of the living, those good things of the Lord

in which she had believed; but for myself I mourn, because so long as I suffer the miseries of this mortal life in the land of the dead, so long am I constrained to exclaim day by day: "Unhappy man that I am, who shall deliver me from the body of this death!" [1]

§ 5. Since, then, I am about to speak of that nobility of the mind which she had in Christ, it is fitting that something should be premised as to her nobility according to this world. Her grandfather was that King Edmund who had earned an honourable surname from his matchless valour, for he was staunch in fight and not to be overcome by his enemies; and therefore he was called in English "The Ironside." His brother on his father's side, but not on his mother's, was the most religious and meek Edward, who proved himself a father to his country, which, like another Solomon (that is, a lover of peace), he protected rather by peace than arms. His was a spirit which overcame anger, despised avarice, and was utterly free from pride. And no wonder; for as from his ancestors he drew the glory of his

[1] Rom. vii. 24.

kingly rank, so from them too he inherited his
nobility of life. He was descended from Edgar,
King of the English, and Richard, Count of the
Normans, his grandfathers on either side; not
only most illustrious, but also most religious men.
Of Edgar it may briefly be said (if we would do
justice to his worth as well in this world as in
Christ), that he was marked out beforehand as a
king at once just and peaceful. For at his birth
St Dunstan heard the holy angels rejoicing in
heaven and singing with great joy: "Let there
be peace, let there be joy in the Church of the
English as long as this new-born child shall hold
his kingdom and Dunstan run the course of this
mortal life."

§ 6. Richard also, father to Emma the mother
of this Edward, was an ancestor worthy of so
illustrious a grandchild; he was a man of energy
and worthy of all praise. None of his forefathers
had attained greater prosperity and honour in his
earldom of Normandy, nor was any of them more
fervent in religion. Though of great wealth, he
was poor in spirit, like a second David; though
raised to be lord over his people, he was the

most humble servant of the servants of Christ.
Among other memorials of his love of religion,
this devout worshipper founded the noble monastery of Fécamp, in which it was his frequent
custom to stay with the religious. There, in
habit a secular but in heart a monk, he placed
the food of the brethren on the table where they
were eating their silent meals and served them
with drink; so that, according to the Scriptures,
"The greater he was, by so much the more did
he humble himself to all." [1] If anyone wishes to
be more fully acquainted with his works of
magnificence and virtue, let him read the book
called "The Acts of the Normans," [2] which con-
tains his history. Edward, the grandchild of
such forefathers, did in no way degenerate from
their renown and excellence. As already has
been said, he was the brother of King Edmund
on the father's side only; from whose son came
Margaret, who by the splendour of her merits
completes the glory of this illustrious pedigree.

§ 7. Whilst Margaret was yet in the flower
of youth, she began to lead a very strict life, to

[1] Eccl. iii. 20.
[2] See Duchesne, "Historiæ Normannorum Scriptores."

love God above all things, to employ herself in the study of the Divine writings, and therein with joy to exercise her mind. Her understanding was keen to comprehend any matter, whatever it might be; to this was joined a great tenacity of memory, enabling her to store it up, along with a graceful flow of language to express it.

§ 8. While thus she was meditating upon the law of the Lord day and night, and, like another Mary sitting at His feet, and delighted to hear His word, rather in obedience to the will of her friends than to her own, yea by the appointment of God, she was married to Malcolm, son of King Duncan, the most powerful king of the Scots. But although she was compelled to do as the world does, she thought it beneath her dignity to fix her affection upon the things of the world, so that good works delighted her more than riches. By means of her temporal possessions she earned for herself the rewards of heaven; for there, where her heart was, she had placed her treasure also. And since before all things she sought the kingdom of God and His justice,[1] the bountiful grace of the Almighty freely

[1] St. Matth. vi. 33.

added to her honours and riches in abundance.
This prudent queen directed all such things as it
was fitting for her to regulate; the laws of the
realm were administered by her counsel; by her
care the influence of religion was extended, and
the people rejoiced in the prosperity of their
affairs. Nothing was firmer than her fidelity,
steadier than her favour, or juster than her de-
cisions; nothing was more enduring than her
patience, graver than her advice, or more pleasant
than her conversation.

§ 9. She had no sooner attained this eminent
dignity, than she built an eternal memorial of her
name and devotion in the place where her nuptials
had been held.[1] The noble church which she
erected there in honour of the Holy Trinity
was to serve a threefold purpose; it was in-
tended for the redemption of the king's soul, for
the good of her own, and for securing to her
children prosperity in this life and in that which is
to come. This church she beautified with rich gifts
of various kinds, amongst which, as is well known,
were many vessels of pure and solid gold for

[1] Dunfermline.

the sacred service of the altar, about which I can speak with the greater certainty since, by the queen's orders, I myself, for a long time, had all of them under my charge. She also placed there a cross of priceless value, bearing the figure of our Saviour, which she had caused to be covered with the purest gold and silver studded with gems, a token even to the present day of the earnestness of her faith. She left proofs of her devotion and fervour in various other churches, as witness the Church of St Andrews, in which is preserved a most beautiful crucifix erected by her there, and to be seen even at the present day. Her chamber was never without such objects, those I mean which appertained to the dignity of the divine service. It was, so to say, a workshop of sacred art : copes for the cantors, chasubles, stoles, altar-cloths, and other priestly vestments and church ornaments, were always to be seen, either already made, of an admirable beauty, or in course of preparation.[1]

[1] Not only in Saxon or Celtic times, but until the Reformation, one of the principal occupations of ladies was to work exquisite vestments for churches, so that the old poet thus addresses them :—

§ 10. These works were entrusted to certain **women-of** noble birth and approved gravity **of** manners, who were thought worthy of a part in the queen's service. No men were admitted among them, with the sole exception of such as she permitted to enter along with herself when she paid the women an occasional visit. There was no giddy pertness among them, no light familiarity between them and the men; for the queen united so much strictness with her sweetness of temper, **so** pleasant was she even in her severity, **that all who waited** upon **her, men as**

> " And ye, lovely ladies,
> With your longe fyngres,
> That ye have silk and sandel
> To sowe when tyme is
> Chesibles for chapelynes,
> Churches to honoure."
>
> (*Vision of* **Piers** *Plowman*, vol. i.
> **p. 117, ed.** Wright).

English ladies were so famous for embroidery in solid gold wire or gold thread, that it was called *Opus Anglicum*. (See Rock's Introduction to "Catalogue of Textile Fabrics in South Kensington Museum," and "Church of our Fathers," vol. ii. p. 276.)

well as women, loved her while they feared her, and in fearing loved her. Thus it came to pass that while she was present no one ventured to utter even one unseemly word, much less to do aught that was objectionable. There was a gravity in her very joy, and something stately in her anger. With her, mirth never expressed itself in fits of laughter, nor did displeasure kindle into fury. Sometimes she chid the faults of others— her own always — with that commendable severity tempered with justice which the Psalmist directs us unceasingly to employ, when he says, "Be ye angry, and sin not." Every action of her life was regulated by the balance of the nicest discretion, which impressed its own distinctive character upon each single virtue. When she spoke, her conversation was seasoned with the salt of wisdom; when she was silent, her silence was filled with good thoughts. So thoroughly did her outward bearing correspond with the staidness of her character that it seemed as if she had been born the pattern of a virtuous life. I may say, in short, every word that she uttered, every act that she performed, shewed that she was meditating upon the things of heaven.

§ 11. Nor was she less careful about her children than she was about herself. She took all heed that they should be well brought up, and especially that they should be trained in virtue. Knowing that it is written: "He that spareth the rod hateth his son,"[1] she charged the governor who had the care of the nursery to curb the children, to scold them, and to whip them whenever they were naughty, as frolicksome childhood will often be. Thanks to their mother's religious care, her children surpassed in good behaviour many who were their elders; they were always affectionate and peaceable among themselves, and everywhere the younger paid due respect to the elder. Thus it was that during the solemnities of the Mass, when they went up to make their offerings after their parents, never on any occasion did the younger venture to precede the elder; the custom being for the elder to go before the younger according to the

---

[1] Prov. xiii. 24.

order of their birth.[1] She frequently called them
to her, and carefully instructed them about Christ
and the things of Christ, as far as their age
would permit, and she admonished them to love
Him always. " O, my children," said she, " fear
the Lord; for they who fear Him shall lack
nothing,[2] and if you love Him, He will give you,
my darlings, prosperity in this life and everlasting
happiness with all the saints." Such were this
mother's wishes for her little ones, such her
admonitions, such her prayers for them, poured
out night and day with tears. She prayed that
they might confess their Maker through the faith
which works by love,[3] that confessing they
might worship Him, worshipping might love Him
in all things and above all things, and loving

---

[1] Royal and noble personages were accustomed to make
their offering at Mass. To do this they left their places, and
advancing to the altar or to the entrance of the chancel, placed
their gift in the hand of the celebrant or of the deacon. On
this subject see " History of the Holy Eucharist in Great
Britain," by Father Bridgett, vol. ii. p. 212 ; " Lay Folk's
Mass Book," edited by Canon Simmons, pp. 231-248.

[2] Psalm xxxiii. 10.

[3] Ep. ad Gal. v. 6.

might attain to the glory of the heavenly
kingdom.[1]

[1] It is owing in great measure to this virtuous education
given by Margaret to her sons that Scotland was governed
for the space of 200 years, by seven excellent kings, that
is, by her three sons, Edgar, Alexander, David, by David's
two grandsons, Malcolm IV. and William, and William's
son and grandson, Alexander II. and III. ; during which
space the nation enjoyed greater happiness than perhaps it
ever did before or after. (Cf. Mr Innes, " Sketches of Scottish History," p. 158 ; Mr Hill Burton, " History of Scotland," vol. ii. pp. 190-198 ; Mr Robertson, " Scotland under
her Early Kings," vol. ii. pp. 171-180.)
Orderic (" Migne," vol. 188, p. 620) wrote panegyrics on
the three brothers, and especially on David ; but it is William
of Malmesbury who is especially emphatic on the unparalleled
purity of life of all three. One child only, Edmund, is
spoken of as falling away from the bright example of his
parent. But Edmund repented sincerely, and became a monk
at Montacute, a monastery founded by William the Conqueror
in Somersetshire. (Cf. " Will. Malms. Gest. Reg. Angl.,"
v. § 400.)
The princesses, Matilda and Mary, were placed by their
uncle Eadgar in the Abbey of Romsey, of which his surviving
sister, Christina, was abbess. A few years later she followed
her aunt Christina to Wilton Abbey, which was the place of
nurture and education for many young princesses of the Anglo-
Saxon royal families.

RUINS OF THE ROYAL PALACE, DUNFERMLINE.

CHAPTER II.

HER CARE FOR THE HONOUR OF THE REALM AND THE DISCIPLINE OF THE CHURCH.

§ 12.

NOR need we wonder that the queen governed herself and her household wisely when we know that she herself acted always under the wisest of masters, the guidance of the Holy Scriptures. I myself have had frequent opportunities of admiring in her how, even amidst the distractions of lawsuits, amidst the countless cares of state, she devoted herself with wonderful assiduity to the word of God, about which she used to ask profound questions from the learned men who were sitting near her. But just as no one among them possessed a deeper intellect than herself, so none had the power of clearer expression. Thus it very often happened that these doctors went from her wiser men by much than when they came. She sought with a religious earnestness for those sacred volumes, and oftentimes her affectionate familiarity with me urged me to exert myself to obtain them for her use.[1] Not that in doing this she cared for her own salvation only; she thought of that of others too.

§ 13. First of all, in regard to King Malcolm: by the help of God she made him most attentive to the works of justice, mercy, almsgiving, and

---

[1] In the Middle Ages the Bible was comparatively seldom formed into one volume, and more commonly existed in its different parts. Even in the earliest periods we meet with notices of translations of numerous portions of the Inspired Writings into the various modern languages, and many copies of these different versions still remain in preservation. We know of translations of the Bible into sixteen modern languages, all made between the fourth and fifteenth centuries; and these must obviously have been made for the use of the laity, since the Scriptures were read by the monks and clergy in Latin, then the universal tongue of learned Christendom. Often, indeed, this purpose was openly avowed. Thus Ælfric avers that he rendered the Scriptures into the vernacular "For the Edification of the Simple, who Know only that Language" (MSS. Camb. Wanley, 153). On this subject see Maitland's celebrated work "The Dark Ages," p. 187, *et seq.* (Cf. L. A. Buckingham's "The Bible in the Middle Ages," L. 1853, p. 45, *et seq.*)

other virtues. From her he learnt how to keep
the vigils of the night in constant prayer; she
instructed him by her exhortation and example
how to pray to God with groanings from the
heart and abundance of tears. I was astonished,
I confess, at this great miracle of God's mercy
when I perceived in the king such a steady
earnestness in his devotion, and I wondered how
it was that there could exist in the heart of a
man living in the world such an entire sorrow
for sin. There was in him a sort of dread of
offending one whose life was so venerable; for
he could not but perceive from her conduct
that Christ dwelt within her; nay, more, he
readily obeyed her wishes and prudent counsels
in all things. Whatever she refused, he refused
also; whatever pleased her, he also loved for the
love of her. Hence it was that, although he
could not read, he would turn over and examine
books which she used either for her devotions or
her study; and whenever he heard her say that
she was fonder of one of them than the others,
this one he too used to look at with special
affection, kissing it, and often taking it into his

hands. Sometimes he sent for a worker in precious metals, whom he commanded to ornament that volume with gold and gems, and when the work was finished, the king himself used to carry the volume to the queen as a kind proof of his devotion.

§ 14. The queen on her side, herself a noble gem of royal race, much more ennobled the splendour of her husband's kingly magnificence, and contributed no little glory and grace to the entire nobility of the realm and their retainers. It was due to her that the merchants who came by land and sea from various countries brought along with them for sale different kinds of precious wares which until then were unknown in Scotland. And it was at her instigation that the natives of Scotland purchased from these traders clothing of various colours, with ornaments to wear; so that from this period, through her suggestion, new costumes of different fashions were adopted, the elegance of which made the wearers appear like a new race of beings.[1] She

[1] Hence, Lord Hailes conjectures that perhaps we owe to her the introduction of what we call Tartan. ("Hailes, Ann. Scot." vol. i. p. 37).

also arranged that a higher class of attendants
should wait upon the king, by a large body of
whom he should be accompanied in great state
whenever he either walked or rode abroad. This
was carried out with such discipline that, wherever
they came, none of them was suffered to take
anything from anyone, nor did they dare in any
way to oppress or injure country people or
the poor. Further, she added to the state
of the royal palace, so that not only was it
brightened by the many-coloured apparel worn
in it, but the whole dwelling blazed with gold
and silver; since the vessels employed for serving
the food and drink to the king and the nobles of
the realm were of gold and silver, or at least
were gilt and plated.

§ 15. All this the queen did, not because the
honours of the world delighted her, but because
duty compelled her to discharge what the kingly
dignity required. For even as she walked in
state, robed in royal splendour, she, like another
Esther, in her heart trod all these trappings under
foot, and bade herself remember that beneath
the gems and gold there was but dust and ashes.

In short, in her exalted dignity she was always
especially watchful to preserve her humility.   It
was easy for her to repress all vain glory arising
from worldly splendour, since her soul never lost
sight of this frail life's transitory nature.   She
always bore in mind that text which describes our
condition in this our unstable humanity : "Man,
born of a woman, living for a short time, is filled
with many miseries. Who cometh forth as a flower
and is destroyed, and fleeth as a shadow, and
never continueth in the same state." [1] She medi-
tated without ceasing upon that passage of the
Blessed Apostle James, who says : "What is our
life? It is a vapour which appeareth for a little
while, and afterwards shall vanish away." [2] And
because, as the Scripture says, "Blessed is the
man that is always fearful," [3] this worthy queen
made it easier for her to shun sin by placing ever
before her soul's eyes, tremblingly and fearfully,
the terrible day of judgment. With this thought
she frequently entreated me to have no hesitation
in rebuking her in private whenever I saw anything worthy of blame either in her words or

[1] Job xiv. 1, 2.   [2] St Jas. iv. 15.   [3] Prov. xxviii. 14.

actions. As I did this less frequently and sharply than she wished, she urged the duty on me, and chid me for being drowsy (so to speak) and negligent towards her ; "for," as she said, "the just man shall correct me in mercy and shall reprove me; but let not the oil," that is, the flattery, "of the sinner fatten my head."[1] "Better are the wounds of a friend than the deceitful kisses of an enemy."[2] She could speak thus because she courted censure as helping to her progress in virtue, where another might have reckoned it a disgrace.

§ 16. Journeying thus onwards towards **the** heavenly country in thought and word and deed, this devout and god-worthy queen called on others to accompany her in the undefiled way, so that they with her might attain true happiness. When she saw wicked men she admonished them to be good, the good to become better, the better to strive **to** be best. The zeal of God's house (that is, of the Church) had so consumed her that with apostolic faith she laboured to root up all weeds which **had** lawlessly sprung up therein. Observing that many practices existed

[1] Ps. cxl. 5.   [2] Prov. xxvii. 6.

among the Scottish nation which were contrary to the rule of the right faith and the holy customs of the universal Church, she caused frequent councils to be held, in order that by some means or other she might, through the gift of Christ, bring back into the way of truth those who had gone astray.

§ 17. Among these councils the most important is that in which for three days she, with a very few of her friends,[1] combated the defenders of a perverse custom with the sword of the Spirit, that is to say, with the word of God.[2] It seemed as if a second Helena were there present, for just as she in former days by citing passages from the Scriptures overcame the Jews, so in our times did this queen those who were in error. In this discussion the king himself took part as an

[1] The names of those friends are not given by Turgot. But we know from other sources that Margaret had requested Lanfranc, Archbishop of Canterbury, to become her spiritual father. In conformity with this solicitation, Lanfranc despatched to her three of his brethren, the senior being the English Goldwine, or Godwin, as the foundation of a renovated establishment. (Letter of Lanfranc to Queen Margaret; "Migne, Patres Latini," Sæc. xi. Col. 549.)

[2] Ep. ad Ephes. vi. 17.

assessor and chief actor, being fully prepared both to say and do whatever she might direct in the matter at issue. And as he knew the English language quite as well as his own, he was in this council a very careful interpreter for either side.

§ 18. The queen introduced the subject under discussion by premising that all who serve one God in one faith along with the Catholic Church ought not to vary from that Church by new or far-fetched usages. She then laid it down, in the first place, that the fast of Lent was not kept as it ought to be by such persons as were in the habit of beginning it on the Monday of the week following, thus differing from the Holy Catholic Church, which begins it on the fourth day of the week at the commencement of Lent. The others objected thus : " The fast which we observe we keep according to the authority of the Gospel, which reports that Christ fasted for six weeks." She replied by saying : " Herein you differ widely from the Gospel, wherein we read that our Lord fasted for forty days, a thing which notoriously you do not do. For seeing that during the six weeks you deduct the six Sundays from the fast, it is clear that thirty-six days only remain on which to fast. Plainly, then, the fast which you keep is not that fast of forty days which is commanded by the Gospel, but consists of six and thirty days only. It comes then to this, you ought to do as we do. Like us, you should begin your fast four days before the commencement of Lent; that is, if you wish, according to our Lord's example, to observe an abstinence of forty days. If you do not do this, you will be the only persons who are acting in opposition to the authority of our Lord Himself and the tradition of the entire Holy Church." Convinced by this plain demonstration of the truth, these persons began henceforth the solemnities of the fasts as Holy Church does everywhere.

§ 19. The queen now raised another point; she asked them to explain why it was that on the festival of Easter they neglected to receive the Sacrament of the Body and Blood of Christ, according to the usage of the Holy and Apostolic Church? They answered her thus: "The Apostle when speaking of persons who eat and drink unworthily, says, that they eat and drink judgment to themselves.[1] Now, since we admit that we are sinners, we fear to approach that mystery, lest we should eat and drink judgment to ourselves." "What!" said the queen to them; "Shall no one that is a sinner taste that holy mystery? If so, then it follows that no one at all should receive it, for no one is pure from sin; no, not even the infant, whose life is but one day upon the earth. And if no one ought to receive it, why did the Lord make this proclamation in the Gospel? 'Except you shall eat the flesh of the Son of Man and drink His Blood, you shall not have life in you.'[2] But if you would understand the passage which you have quoted from the Apostle according to the interpretation of the Fathers, then you must give it quite a different meaning. The Evangelist does not hold that all sinners are unworthy of the sacraments of salvation; for after saying 'He eateth and drinketh judgment to himself,' he adds, 'Not discerning the Body of the Lord;'[3] that is, not distinguishing it by faith from bodily

---

[1] 1 Cor. xi. 29. [2] St John vi. 54.
[3] 1 Cor. xi. 29.

food. It is the man who, without confession and
penance, but carrying with him the defilements of
his sins presumes to approach the sacred mys-
teries, such an one, I say it is, who eats and
drinks judgment to himself. Whereas we who
many days previously have made confession of
our sins and have been cleansed from their stains
by chastening penance, by trying fasts, by almsgiving and tears—approaching in the Catholic
faith to the Lord's Table on the day of His
Resurrection, receive the Body and Blood of
Jesus Christ, the immaculate Lamb, not to judgment but to the remission of our sins, and as a
health-giving preparation for eternal happiness."
To these arguments they could not answer a word,
and knowing now the meaning of the Church's
practices, observed them ever after in the sacrament
of salvation.

§ 20. Again, there were certain places in Scotland in which Masses were celebrated according
to some sort of barbarous rite, contrary to the
usage of the whole Church. Fired by the zeal
of God, the Queen attempted to root out and
abolish this custom, so that henceforth, from the

whole of Scotland, there was not one single
person who dared to continue the practice.[1]

It was another custom of **theirs to neglect
the reverence due to the Lord's Day** by
devoting themselves **to** every kind of worldly

---

[1] Turgot, unfortunately, does **not** say in what the barbarousness of the rites consisted. On this subject, says the late Dr Forbes, we cannot do better than quote the words of that learned antiquary, the Right Reverend Bishop Kyle: "The contemporary biographer of St Margaret tells us that certain priests in Scotland followed, in celebrating Mass, **a rite which** to him and the Queen appeared barbarous: which rite **she** laboured so effectually to abolish, that none in Scotland in his time adhered to it." **I** suspect that in this last point he **was** mistaken. For **we** learn that the Keledei (*Cele De*, one **who** has devoted himself to the service of God), long after St Margaret's days, were permitted to observe in their **own** churches or chapels a rite different from what was followed by the rest of the Scottish clergy. The rite of the Keledei was probably the **same** with **that** which St Margaret wished to bring into conformity with **the** general use of the Western Church; but neither **her** biographer nor **the chronicles of the** Culdean **observance give us** the least hint wherein **its** peculiarity consisted. (**Lib.** Ecclesiæ B. Terrenani de Arbuthnot, p. liv.) There is no mention of Culdees in Scotland until the ninth century, **as** Chalmers testifies. They were secular canons who had been established since the ninth century. **But** although they were **for the** most **part** clerics, the name seems to have been given also to pious, unmarried laymen, inasmuch **as they** formed a community, and lived together. The later

business upon it just as they did upon other days. That this was contrary to the law, she proved to them as well by reason as by authority. " Let us venerate the Lord's Day," said she, " because of the resurrection of our Lord, which happened upon that day, and let us no longer do servile works upon it ; bearing in mind that upon this day we were redeemed from the slavery of the devil. The blessed Pope Gregory affirms the same, saying : ' We must cease from earthly labour upon the Lord's Day and we must devote ourselves entirely to prayer, so that upon the day of our Lord's resurrection we may make expiations for such negligences as we may have committed during the six days.' "[1] The same Father, Gregory, after censuring with the greatest severity a certain piece of worldly business which had been done on the Lord's Day,

Bollandists have likewise come to the conclusion that they were secular canons or brothers, and appeared, at soonest, in the year 800. (Bollandists, vol. viii., Oct., p. 86 : Disquisitio in Culdæos, cf. Dr Reeves, "The Culdees of the British Islands," Dublin, 1864.)

[1] "Ep. S. Gregorii Magni," lib. xiii., c. 1 opp. ii. p. 1214, ed. Bened.

decreed that the persons who had advised it should be excommunicated for two months. These arguments of the queen were unanswerable ; and from this time forward these prudent men paid such respect to her earnestness that no one dared on these days either to carry any burdens himself or to compel another to do so.

§ 21. Next, she proved how utterly abominable, yea more to be shunned by the faithful than death itself, was the unlawful marriage of a man with his step-mother, as also that the surviving brother should take to wife the widow of his deceased brother; both of which customs had heretofore prevailed in this country. In this council she succeeded in condemning and expelling from her realm many other inveterate abuses which had gained a footing herein, contrary to the Rule of Faith and the institutions and observances of the Church. For everything that she proposed she supported so strongly by the testimonies of the Sacred Scriptures and the teaching of the holy Fathers, that no one on the opposite side could say one word against them ;

nay, rather, giving up their obstinacy and yield-
ing to reason, they willingly consented to adopt
all she recommended.[1]

[1] Even the smallest circumstances of every-day life were
sought out by St Margaret and put to spiritual profit. Having
observed that many neglected to give due thanks to God after
meals, she introduced the practice of drinking a health at rising
from table to those who had complied with that duty. Hence
it was called the *Grace Drink*, or St Margaret's Blessing.

A similar custom is related in some Anglo-Saxon chronicles.
On high festivals and other solemn occasions, to the abbot or
prior of the monastery there was brought a large bowl filled
with wine, of which he drank a little, and handed this
"poculum charitatis," or love-cup, to his monks, each of
whom took a short draught in a like manner: after this cere-
mony, which was meant as a symbol of brotherly affection and
good will one towards another, was said grace, which finished
with a prayer for their benefactors alive and dead (Cod. Dip.
Anglo Sax. v. iv., p. 304). A shadow of this Anglo-Saxon
custom may yet be seen in the grace-cup of the universities,
and the loving-cup passed round among the guests at the great
dinners given by the Lord Mayor of London.

Not many years ago, in Germany as well as Belgium, this
custom was still kept up, of sending round the loving-cup at
grace after dinner. (Cf. Rock, "The Church of our Fathers,"
vol. ii., p. 335 *et seq.*)

CHAPTER III.

HER PIETY; HER CHARITY TO THE POOR; HER
REDEMPTION OF ENGLISH CAPTIVES; HER
MANNER OF PASSING LENT; HER BOOK OF
THE GOSPELS.

§ 22.

HUS it came to pass that this venerable Queen, who (by God's help), had been so desirous to cleanse His house from all filth and error, was found day by day worthier of becoming His temple, as the Holy Spirit shone ever brighter in her heart. And I know of a truth that she was such, because I not only saw the works which she did outwardly, but besides this, I knew her conscience, for to me she revealed it. It was her good pleasure to converse with me on the most familiar terms, and to open her secret thoughts to me; not because there was anything that was good in me, but because

she thought there was. When she spoke with
me about the salvation of the soul and the sweetness of the life which is eternal, every word she
uttered was so filled with grace that the Holy
Spirit, Who truly dwelt within her breast, evi-
dently spoke by her lips. So deep was her con-
trition that whilst she was talking, she seemed as
if she could melt away in tears, so that my soul,
pierced like her own, wept also. Of all living
persons whom I know or have known she was the
most devoted to prayer and fasting, to works of
mercy and almsgiving.

§ 23. Let me speak first of all about her prayer-
fulness. In church no one was so silent and com-
posed as she, no one so wrapt in prayer. Whilst
she was in the house of God she would never speak
of worldly matters, or do anything which savoured
of the earth ; she was there simply to pray, and in
praying to pour forth her tears. Only her body
was then here below, her spirit was near to God,
for in the purity of her prayer she sought nothing
but God and the things which are God's. As
for her fasting, I will say this alone, that the
strictness of her abstinence brought upon her a
very severe infirmity.

§ 24. To these two excellent gifts of prayer and abstinence she joined the gift of mercy. For what could be more compassionate than her heart? Who could be more gentle than she towards the necessitous? Not only would she have given to the poor all that she possessed; but if she could have done so, she would have given her **very self away.** She was poorer than any of her paupers; for they, even when they had nothing, wished to have something; while her anxiety was all to strip herself of what she had. When she went out of doors, either on foot or on horseback, crowds of poor people, orphans and widows flocked to her, as they would have done to a most loving mother, none of whom left her without being comforted. But when she had distributed all she had brought with her for the benefit of the needy, the rich who accompanied her, or her own attendants, used to hand to her their garments, or anything else they happened to have by them at the time, that she might give them to those who were in want; for she was anxious that none of them should go away in distress. Nor were her attendants at all offended

nay rather each strove who should first offer her
what he had, since he knew for certain that she
would pay it back two-fold.   Now and then she
helped herself to something or other out of the
King's private property, it mattered not what it
was, to give to a poor person; and this pious
plundering the King always took pleasantly and
in good part.   It was his custom to offer certain
coins of gold upon Maundy Thursday and at
High Mass, some of which coins the Queen
often devoutly pillaged, and bestowed on the
beggar who was petitioning her for help.   Although the King was fully aware of the theft, he
generally pretended to know nothing of it, and
felt much amused by it.   Now and then he caught
the Queen in the very act, with the money in her
hand, and laughingly threatened that he would
have her arrested, tried, and found guilty.   Nor
was it towards the poor of her own nation only
that she exhibited the abundance of her cheerful
and open-hearted charity, but those persons who
came from almost every other nation, drawn by
the report of her liberality, were the partakers of
her bounty.   Of a truth then this text may be

applied to her, "He hath dispersed abroad, he hath given to the poor, therefore his justice remaineth for ever."[1]

§ 25. But who can tell the number of English of all ranks, carried captive from their own land by violence of war and reduced to slavery,[2] whom she restored to liberty by paying their ransom? Spies were employed by her to go secretly through all the provinces of Scotland and ascertain what captives were oppressed with the most cruel bondage, and treated with the greatest inhumanity. When she had privately ascertained where these prisoners were detained, and by whom ill-treated, commiserating them from the bottom of her heart, she took care to send them speedy help, she paid their ransom and set them at liberty forthwith.

[1] Ps. cxi. 9.

[2] So great was the desolation of England after the conquest, that many became slaves to any one who would feed them. Remigius, Bishop of Lincoln, and St Wulfstan, Bishop of Worcester, preached against the wicked custom by which men sold their country-folk, sometimes their kinsfolk, to a life of shame or of bondage in foreign lands. (Giraldus, "Vita Rem." c. 3, 4, 5.) The slave trade was severely condemned by the council of London in 1103. ("Mausi Collectio Concil.," xx. p. 1152.)

§ 26. At the period of which we are speaking, there were in many places throughout the realm of Scotland persons shut up in different cells, and leading lives of great strictness; in the flesh, but not according to the flesh; for being upon earth, they led the life of angels. These the Queen busied herself in often visiting and conversing with, for in them she loved and venerated Christ, and would recommend herself to their prayers. As she could not induce them to accept any earthly gift from her, she urgently entreated them to be so good as to bid her perform some alms-deed or work of mercy, and this devout woman did forthwith fulfil whatever was their pleasure, either by helping the poor out of their poverty, or by relieving the distressed in their troubles, whatever these might be.[1]

[1] Some of these Anchorites were her own Saxon country-men, driven by the Norman conqueror into exile. Although seclusion and continual prayer have been practised by Christians in all ages since the commencement of the Church, yet the eremitical life has assumed its external form principally by means of persecutions. Like the days of which the Apostle wrote to the Hebrews, "they wandered about in sheep-skins, in goat-skins, being in want, distressed, afflicted, of whom the world was not worthy : wandering in deserts, in mountains, and

§ 27. Since the church **of St** Andrews **was**
much frequented by the devout, who flocked to it
from all quarters, she erected dwellings on either
shore of the sea which divides Lothian from Scotland, so that the poor people and the pilgrims
might shelter there and rest themselves after the
fatigues of their journey. She had arranged that
they should there find all that they needed for
the refreshment of the body. Servants were
appointed, whose especial duty it **was to see that**

in dens, and **in caves of the earth,"** (Heb. **xi.** 37.) Many
who thus began this life under compulsion found **so great a**
sweetness in uninterrupted intercourse with God, and in **the**
perfect subjection of the body to the soul, that they clung
to it when they might have returned to an easier mode of life.
"It is probable that among those Anchorites who commended
themselves so much to her favour were the *Cele De* of Lochleven, for we find Malcolm and Margaret, king and queen
of Scotia, giving devoutly the town of Ballechristin to God
the Omnipotent and the *Keledei* of Louchleven, with the
same liberties as before.* Bishop Fothad too, here called
Modach, son of Malmy Kel, a man of most pious memory,
bishop of St Andrews, with whose life and doctrine the whole
region of the Scots was happily enlightened, gives to God and
St Servanus and the hermit *Keledei* on the island of Lochleven,
living there in the school of all virtues, devoutly and **honour-**
ably, with the same liberties, the church of Auchterderran." †

* Chart. Prior, S.A., p. 115.
† *Ibid*, p. 117, W F. Skene. Celtic Scotland, Vol. II., p 351.

everything that might be required for these way-
farers should be always in readiness, and they
were directed to attend upon them with all dili-
gence. Moreover, she provided ships for the
transport of these pilgrims both coming and going,
nor was it lawful to demand any fee for the
passage from those who were crossing.

§ 28. Having spoken of the daily manner of
life of this venerable queen, as well as of her
daily works of mercy, it is fitting that I should
now attempt to say a few words as to the way in
which she habitually spent the forty days before
Christmas, and the entire season of Lent. After
taking rest for a short period at the beginning of the night, she went into the church,
and there, alone, she completed first of all the
Matins of the Holy Trinity, then the Matins of
the Holy Cross, and lastly the Matins of Our
Lady. Having ended these, she began the offices
of the Dead, and after these the Psalter; nor did
she cease until she had reached its conclusion.
When the Priests were saying the Matins and
Lauds at the fitting hour, she in the meantime
either finished the Psalter she had begun, or if she

had completed it, began saying it a second time.
When the office of Matins and Lauds was finished,
she, returning to her chamber, along with the
King himself, washed the feet of six poor persons;
and used to give them something wherewithal
to relieve their poverty. It was the chamber-
lain's special duty to bring these poor people in
every night before the Queen's arrival, so that
she might find them ready when she came to
wait upon them. Having done this, she went to
take some rest and sleep.

§ 29. When it was morning she rose from
bed and devoted a considerable time to prayer
and the reading of the Psalms, and while reading the Psalms she performed the following work
of mercy. She ordered that nine little orphans
utterly destitute should be brought in to her at
the first hour of the day, and that some soft food
such as children at that tender age like, should
daily be prepared for them. When the little ones
were carried to her she did not think it beneath
her to take them upon her knee, and to get their
pap ready for them, and this she put into their
mouths with the spoon which she herself used.

The queen, who was honoured by all the people, did this act of charity for the sake of Christ, and as one of Christ's servants. To this most loving mother might be applied with great propriety that saying of the blessed Job, "From my infancy mercy grew with me, and it came forth with me from my mother's womb."[1]

§ 30. While this was going on, it was the custom to bring three hundred poor people into the royal hall, and when they had been seated round it in order the king and queen entered; whereupon the doors were shut by the servants; for with the exception of the chaplains, certain religious, and a few attendants, no one was permitted to be present at their alms-deeds.[2]

[1] Job xxxi. 18.

[2] That this access to her might be easier, she is said to have frequently sat in an open field, where every one who pleased might have an opportunity of speaking to her with greater freedom; and there is still shown, on the road to Queensferry, rather more than a mile from Dunfermline, a stone in the form of a seat, which, according to a constant tradition, she sometimes made use of for that purpose. It is marked in the maps of the roads published not long since, as being near the fourteenth mile from Edinburgh, with the name of *St Margaret's Stone* affixed to it. ("The Life of St Margaret," by the Right Rev. T. Geddes, Aberdeen, 1794, p. 34.)

The king on the one side and the queen on the
other waited upon Christ in the person of His
poor, and served them with food and drink which
had been prepared for this special purpose.
When this was finished, the queen's custom
was to go into the church, and there with long
prayers, with tears and sighs to offer herself as
a sacrifice to God. Upon holy days, in addition
to the hours of the Holy Trinity, the Holy Cross,
and Holy Mary, recited within the space of a day
and a night, she used to repeat the Psalter twice or
thrice ; and before the celebration of the Public
Mass she caused five or six Masses to be sung
privately in her presence.

§ 31. When these were finished, meal-time
was at hand. But before it was served she
herself humbly waited upon twenty-four poor
people whom she fed ; for without reckoning any
of the alms-deeds which I have already mentioned,
throughout the course of the year she supported
twenty-four poor as long as she lived. It was
her will that wherever she lived they also should
be living in the neighbourhood ; wherever she
went they were to accompany her. Not until

after she had devoutly waited upon Christ in these His poor was it her habit to refresh her own feeble body. In this meal she hardly allowed herself the necessaries of life, since the Apostle teaches us that we ought not to make provision for the flesh in its concupiscences.[1] She ate no more than sufficed for the preservation of her life, and not to gratify her palate. Her meal—frugal and scanty—rather excited hunger than allayed it. She seemed to taste her food, not to take it. From this let it be understood, I pray you, how great was her abstinence when she fasted, remembering what it was when she feasted. Her whole life was one of exceeding temperance, but during the fasts (that is for the forty days before Easter and Christmas), the abstinence she was accustomed to afflict herself with was incredible. By reason of this excessive severity she suffered to the end of her life from an acute pain in the stomach; yet the weakness of the body did not impair her virtue in good works. During this period she was assiduous in reading the sacred volumes, she was instant in prayer, her

---

[1] Rom. xiii. 14.

alms were unceasing, and she exercised herself wholly and watchfully in all the things of God. And knowing, as she did, that it is written: "Whom the Lord loveth he chastiseth, and He scourgeth every son whom He receiveth,"[1] she willingly accepted with patience and thanksgiving the pains of the flesh, regarding them as the stripes of a most loving Father.

§ 33. Devoted as she was to such works as these, and burdened by the like constant infirmities, God's power was made perfect in her weakness.[2] Thus passing onwards from strength to strength, each day made her better. And now forsaking all things earthly with her whole soul, she longed for the things of heaven, yea, thirsted after them, exclaiming with the Psalmist in the language both of her heart and lips, " My soul hath thirsted after God, the living fountain ; when shall I come and appear before the face of God ? "[3] I leave it to others to admire the tokens of miracles which they see elsewhere, I admire much more the works of mercy which I perceived in Margaret ; for signs are common to

[1] Prov. iii. 11, 12.   [2] 2 Cor. xii. 9.   [3] Ps. xli. 3.

the good and the bad, whereas works of piety and true charity belong to the good only. The former sometimes are the proof of holiness, the latter are that which constitutes it. Let us then, I repeat, admire in Margaret the actions which made her a saint, rather than the miracles which, had we any record of them, would have proved that she was one. In her character let us observe with admiration the works of the ancient Saints rather than their miracles — her justice, her piety, her mercy, and her love. Yet it will not be out of place if I here narrate one incident which may go to prove what the holiness of her life was.

§ 33. She had a book of the Gospels beautifully adorned with gold and precious stones, and ornamented with the figures of the four Evangelists, painted and gilt. All the capital letters throughout the volume were radiant with gold. She had always felt a particular attachment for this book; more so than for any of the others which she usually read. It happened that as the person who carried it was once crossing a ford, he let the book, which had been carelessly folded in a wrapper, fall into the middle of the stream. Unconscious of what had occurred the man quietly continued his journey; but when he wished to produce the book, suddenly it dawned upon him that he had lost it. Long was it sought, but nowhere could it be found. At last it was discovered lying open at the bottom of the river. Its leaves had been kept in constant motion by the action of the water, and the little coverings of silk which protected the letters of gold from becoming injured by contact with the leaves, were swept away by the force of the current. Who could have imagined that the book was worth anything after such an accident as this? Who could have believed that so much as a single letter would have been visible. Yet of a truth, it was taken up from the middle of the river so perfect, so uninjured, so free from damage that it looked as if it had not been touched by the water. The whiteness of the leaves and the form of the letters throughout the volume continued exactly as they had been before it had fallen into the stream, except that on the margin of the leaves, towards the edge, the least possible mark of

water might be detected. The book was conveyed to the queen, and the miracle was reported
to her at the same time; and she, having thanked
Christ, valued it much more highly than she had ⸱
done before. Whatever others may think, I
for my part believe that this wonder was worked
by our Lord out of His love for this venerable
queen.

THE FRATER HALL, DUNFERMLINE ABBEY.

CHAPTER IV.

§ 34.

WHILST Almighty God was preparing everlasting rewards for her works of devotion, the queen was preparing herself with more than her usual assiduity for entering another life. Her own words made this more obvious shortly afterwards. It would seem that her own departure from this world, as well as certain other events which were impending, were known by her long beforehand. Therefore, summoning me to come to her privately, she began to recount to me in order the history of her life, and as she proceeded with it she shed floods of tears. In short, so deep was her compunction, and out of this compunction sprang such abundant tears, that—as it seemed to me—

there was nothing whatever which at that time she might not have obtained from Christ. When she wept, I wept likewise; and thus we wept and at times were silent altogether, since by reason of our sobs we could not give utterance to words. For the flame of that compunction which consumed her heart reached my soul also, borne in thither by the spiritual fervour of her words. And when I heard the language of the Holy Ghost speaking by her tongue, and could thoroughly read the tenderness of her conscience by what she said, I judged myself unworthy of the grace of so exalted a familiarity.[1]

§ 35. When she had ended what she had to say about matters which were pressing, she then addressed herself to me, saying: "I now bid you farewell. I shall not continue much longer in this world, but you will live after me for a consider-

[1] Instead of the above paragraph, Capgrave's abridgment of this biography, printed also by Surius, has as follows: "Habebat confessarium Turgotum, secundum Priorem Dunelmiæ. Illi ergo ad se accersito, vitam suam replicare cæpit, et ad singula verba lachrymarum flumina profundere; tantaque erat sub ejus sermonibus compunctio, tantus lachrymarum imber, ut nihil proculdubio esse videretur, quod tunc a Christo impetrare non posset." This is copied by Pinkerton, p. 381.

able time. There are two things which I beg of
you. One is, that as long as you survive you
will remember me in your prayers; the other is,
that you will take some care about my sons and
daughters. Lavish your affection upon them;
teach them before all things to love and fear
God; never cease instructing them. When you
see any one of them exalted to the height of an
earthly dignity, then, as at once his father and
his master in the truest sense, go to him, warn
him lest through means of a passing honour he
become puffed up with pride, or offend God by
avarice, or through prosperity in this world
neglect the blessedness of the life which is eternal. These are the things, said she, which I
ask you—as in the sight of God, who now is
present along with us two—to promise me that
you will carefully perform. At these words, I
once more burst into tears, and promised her
that I would carefully perform her wishes; for I
did not dare to oppose one whom I heard thus
unhesitatingly predict what was to come to pass.
And the truth of her prediction is verified by
present facts; since I survive her death, and I see

her offspring elevated to dignity and honour. Thus, having ended the conference, and being about to return home, I bade the queen my last farewell; for after that day I never saw her face in the flesh.

§ 36. Shortly afterwards she was attacked by an infirmity of unusual severity, and was purified by the fire of a tedious sickness before the day on which God called her to Himself. I will describe her death as I heard it narrated by a priest of hers, whom she loved more intimately than the others on account of his simplicity, his innocence, and his purity. After the queen's death he made an oblation in perpetual service for her soul, and having put on the monk's habit offered himself up as a sacrifice for her at the tomb of the uncorrupt body of the most holy Father Cuthbert. He was continually with the queen during the last days of her life, and with his prayers recommended her soul to Christ when it was leaving the body. He gave me more than once a connected history of her decease as he saw it, for I frequently asked him to do so; and he did this with tears.

§ 37. "For a little more than half a year," said he, "she was never able to ride on horseback, seldom to rise from her bed. On the fourth day preceding her death, while the king was absent on an expedition, and at such a great distance that it was impossible for any messenger, however swift he might be, to bring her tidings of what was happening to him, she became sadder than usual. Then she said to me, for I was seated near her, 'Perhaps on this very day such a heavy calamity may befall the realm of Scotland as has not been for many ages past.' When I heard these words I paid no great attention to them, but a few days afterwards a messenger arrived who told us that the king was slain on the very day on which the queen had spoken the words narrated. As if foreseeing the future, she had been most urgent with him not to go with the army, but it came to pass—how I know not—that he did not follow her advice.[1]

---

[1] We have no very clear account of the immediate cause which led to the open breach between William and Malcolm. But it is plain from the Peterborough Chronicle that William was in the wrong; he refused to do something for Malcolm which he had promised to do. Malcolm entered the earldom

§ 38. "On the approach of the fourth day after the king's death, her weakness having somewhat

of Northumberland, and ravaged after his usual fashion as far as some point which, there is no reason to doubt, was in the near neighbourhood of **Alnwick**. We may fairly accept the tradition which carries him to the spot known as Malcolm's Cross, where a commemorative rood was erected, and where the ruins of a Romanesque chapel may still be seen. The spot is on high ground overlooking the river Alne, while on the opposite side of the stream a lower height is crowned by the town of Alnwick, and by such remains of its famous castle as modern innovation has spared. By ambush or some other stratagem **Earl Robert** of Mowbray led his forces against the Scottish king unawares, under circumstances which are not detailed, but which have led even English writers to speak of the attack as treacherous. Malcolm was killed ; and with him died his son and expected heir, Edward. The actual slayer of Malcolm was his gossip Morel, Earl Robert's nephew and steward, guardian of the rock and fortress of Bambrough.* Simeon of Durham says that he was cut off near the river Alne, and that "part of his army fell by the sword, and part escaping the sword were carried away by the inundation of the rivers, then more than usually swollen by the winter rains. Two of the natives placed the body of the king in a cart, as none of his men were left to commit it to the ground, and buried it at Tynemouth. † Thus terminated his long reign of thirty-five years." ‡

* E. Freeman, "The Reign of William Rufus," vol. ii. p. 15.

† Sim. Dun. de Gest. Reg. ad an. 1093. By some of the Scotch chronicles Malcolm is said to have been slain at Inneraldan, by others at Alnwick.

‡ Malcolm Ceanmor reigned from the 17th March 1057-8 to the 13th Nov. 1093, the day on which he was slain.

abated, the queen **went into her** oratory **to hear**
Mass ; and there she took care **to** provide herself
beforehand for her departure, which **was now so**
near, with the holy Viaticum of the Body and
Blood of our Lord. Having partaken of this
health-giving food, she returned to her bed, for
her former pains assailed her with redoubled

The character of Malcolm was variously regarded by the
English and by his own subjects. The English historians,
who had mainly to record his frequent invasions **of** Northum-
berland, regarded him as a man of barbarous disposition,
delighting, at the instigation of his avarice, to ravage and de-
vastate the northern districts of England ; while they attributed
any better traits in his character to the humanising influence of
his consort Queen Margaret. By his Celtic subjects he was
known as Malcolm Ceanmor, or great head, and was regarded,
according to the testimony of St Berchan, as

> " A king, the best who possessed Alban ;
> He was a king of kings fortunate.
> He was the vigilant crusher of enemies.
> No woman bore or will bring forth in the East
> A king whose rule will be greater over Alban ;
> And there shall not be born for ever
> One who had more fortune and greatness."

On his death he left the kingdom in possession for the first
time of the same southern frontier which it ever after re-
tained.[*]

[*] F. Skene, " Celtic Scotland," vol. i. pp. 431, 432.

severity. The disease gained ground, and death was imminent. . . . Her face had already grown pallid in death when she directed that I, and the other ministers of the sacred Altar along with me, should stand near her and commend her soul to Christ by our psalms. Moreover, she asked that there should be brought to her a cross, called the Black Cross,[1] which she always held in the greatest veneration. There was some delay in opening the chest in which it was kept, during which the queen, sighing deeply, exclaimed, 'O unhappy that we are! O guilty that we are! Shall we not be permitted once more to look upon the Holy Cross!' When at last it was got out of the chest and brought to her, she received it with reverence, and did her best to embrace it and kiss it, and several times she signed herself with it. Although every part of her body was now growing cold, still as long as the warmth of life throbbed at her heart she continued steadfast in prayer. She repeated the whole of the Fiftieth Psalm, and placing the cross

[1] "Crucem Scotiæ nigram," Brit. Mus. MS. Tiberius, E. i., 186a.

before her eyes, she held it there with both her
hands.[1]

§ 39. "It was at this point that her son,[2] who
now, after his father, holds in this realm the reins
of government, having returned from the army,
entered the queen's bedroom. Conceive his
distress at this moment ! Imagine to yourself
how his heart was racked ! He stood there in a
strait ; everything was against him, and whither

[1] The Black Cross was enclosed in a black case, from
whence it was called *the Black Cross.* The cross itself was
of gold, and set with large diamonds. "It is about an ell
long," says Aelred, "manufactured of pure gold, of most
wonderful workmanship, and is shut and opened like a
chest. Inside may be seen a portion of our Lord's Cross
(as has often been proved by convincing miracles), having
a figure of our Saviour sculptured of massive ivory, and
marvellously adorned with gold. Queen Margaret had
brought this with her to Scotland, and handed it down as
an heirloom to her sons ; and the youngest of them, David,
when he became king, built a magnificent church for it near the
city, called Holy-Rood." (Bollandists, vol. xxi. p. 335.)
When Edward the First invaded Scotland, he seized on
this cross as one of the English crown jewels, and carried it into
England. Robert Bruce so vehemently insisted on its restoration that Queen Isabella yielded it up on the pacification during
her regency in 1327 ; but its surrender exasperated the English
more than the most flagrant of her misdeeds.

[2] Filius suus Edgarus. MS. Tiberius, E. i., 186.

to turn himself he knew not.   He had come to announce to his mother that his father and brother were slain, and he found his mother, whom he loved most dearly, at the point of death.   He knew not whom first to lament.   Yet the loss of his dearest mother, whom he saw lying nearly dead before his eyes, stung him to the heart with the keenest pang.   Besides all this, the condition of the realm occasioned him the deepest anxiety, for he was fully aware that there would be an insurrection upon the death of his father.   Sadness and trouble beset him on every side.

§ 40.   "The queen, who, as it seemed to the by-standers, was rapt in an agony, suddenly rallied her strength and spoke to her son.   She asked him about his father and his brother.   He was unwilling to tell the truth, and fearing that if she heard of their death she herself would immediately die, he replied that they were well.   But with a deep sigh she said, 'I know it, my boy, I know it. By this holy cross, by the bond of our blood, I adjure you to tell me the truth.'   Thus pressed, he told her exactly all that had happened.   What could she do, think you?   To murmur against

God with such a one was impossible. At the
same moment she had lost her husband and her
son, and disease was putting her to a cruel death,
but in all these things she sinned not with her
lips, nor spoke foolishly against God. Raising
her eyes and her hands towards heaven, she
glorified God, saying, 'I give praise and thanks
to Thee, Almighty God, for that Thou hast been
pleased that I should endure such deep sorrow
at my departing, and I trust that by means of this
suffering it is Thy pleasure that I should be
cleansed from some of the stains of my sins.'

§ 41. "Feeling now that death was close at
hand, she at once began the prayer which is
usually said by the priest before he receives the
Body and Blood of our Lord, saying, 'Lord Jesus
Christ, who according to the will of the Father,
through the co-operation of the Holy Ghost, hast
by Thy death given life to the world, deliver me.
As she was saying the words, 'Deliver me,' her
soul was freed from the chains of the body, and
departed to Christ, the author of true liberty, to
Christ whom she had always loved, and by whom
she was made a partaker of the happiness of the

saints, the example of whose virtues she had
followed. Her departure was so calm, so tran-
quil, that we conclude her soul passed to the
land of eternal rest and peace. It was remark-
able that her face, which, when she was dying
had exhibited the usual pallor of death, became
afterwards suffused with red and white tints, so
that it seemed as if she were not dead but sleep-
ing.[1] Her corpse was shrouded as became a
queen, and we carried her to the Church of the

---

[1] The place of her death is not mentioned by Turgot in the
Life. According to Fordun (v. 21), Margaret died in Edinburgh "in castro puellarum;" on the 16th of November in the
year 1093, according to the Chronicle of Mailros. See also
the Surtees "Simeon," p. 262. Wynton relates the occurrence
as follows :—

> "As thys dede all thys ware doune
> Come wything til Saynt Margret soune
> The Revelatyoune that west maist,
> That scho had of the Haly Gast.
> Than wyth devot and gud intent
> Scho tuk the Haly Sacrament
> Of Goddis Body blyst wërray
> Wyth the last unctyoune ; and that dai
> Of al charges scho yhald hyr gwyte
> And til the Creatoure hyr Spyryte
> In-til the Castelle of Edynburgh," etc.

(Wynton's "Orygynale Cronikil," vol. ii. pp. 271, 272.)

Holy Trinity,[1] which she had built. There, as she herself had directed, we committed it to the grave, opposite the altar and the venerable sign of the Holy Cross which she had erected. And thus her body at length rests in that place in which, when alive, she used to humble herself with vigils, prayers, and tears."

END OF TURGOT'S LIFE.

———————

The public opinion of Margaret's sanctity had already prevailed all over Britain for the space of more than one hundred and fifty years, when it received the sanction of Pope Innocent IV. in the year 1250. On that occasion, and on the 19th of June of that year, the body of the saint was taken up from the grave, where it had hitherto lain, and was put into a silver shrine, adorned with precious stones, which was placed under the high altar of the church.[2]

[1] Dunfermline Abbey.   [2] Brev. Abd., 19 Jun.

"According to Papebroch's appendix to the life of the saint and queen, her head was brought to the Castle of Edinburgh at the desire of Queen Mary, who was in it at the time, and on her flight into England in 1567 it was removed to the house of the Laird of Dury, where it was preserved for many years by a Benedictine monk, but in the year 1597 was by him given up to the missionary Jesuits. One of these, John Robie, conveyed it to Antwerp. There John Malder, Bishop of Antwerp, after proper examination, issued his letters, on 15th September 1620, authenticating the head as that of St Margaret, and granting leave for its being exposed to public veneration. After seven years the relic was translated to the Scots College at Douay, where, by permission of Herman, Bishop of Arras, and his successor, Paul Boudot, it was again exposed as a genuine relic to public veneration. Pope Innocent X., by a brief dated March 4th, 1645, granted a plenary indulgence to those who should visit the church of the college on the festival of St Margaret, and this grant was confirmed by his successors at various times afterwards. It is believed that this relic disappeared amid the commotions of the French Revolution.[1]

"With regard to the other remains of Queen Margaret and her husband, if we may believe the accounts given by Papebroch, which he seems to have partly, if not wholly, derived from a statement by George Con, in his treatise, 'De Duplice Statu Religionis apud Scotos,' they were, after much labour, acquired by Philip II., King of Spain, and by him placed in the Church of St Lawrence at the Escurial, with the inscriptions, 'St Malcolm, King; St Margaret, Queen,' on the urns containing them. Bishop Gillis, in the hope of having the relics of St Margaret again restored to a Scottish shrine, invoked the aid of Pius the Ninth in an application to the Spanish Government for their restoration, but they could not be found, or at all events identified."[2]

[1] In 1785 it was still at Douay, where the historian Carruthers saw it at the Scotch College. It was in extraordinary preservation, with a quantity of fine hair, fair in colour, still upon it.

[2] "Transactions of the Antiquarian Society of Scotland," ii. 89. Cf. Bishop Challoner, "Britannia Sancta"; Alban Butler, "Lives of the Saints," vol. vi., June 10, Edinburgh edition, 1709, p. 154.

www.ingramcontent.com/pod-product-compliance
Lightning Source LLC
Chambersburg PA
CBHW032356020726
47499CB00008B/2778